The stories of Aladdin and Ali Baba are taken from a collection of stories called The Thousand and One Nights. These stories are based on ancient Persian, Arabian and Indian tales handed down by word of mouth for hundreds of years. They first appeared in their present form, in Arabic, in 1450. The tales are linked together by the story of Sheherazade.

Sheherazade was the wife of the Sultan and had been condemned to death for her wickedness. She managed to put off her execution by telling one of the stories to her sister each night, in the presence of the Sultan. Being a very clever woman, as well as a talented storyteller, Sheherazade always left the most exciting part of the story until the following night. The Sultan could not bear to miss the end of each story, and kept on putting off the execution. For a thousand and one nights Sheherazade kept the Sultan spellbound with the stories. He eventually realised that he had been wrong and forgave Sheherazade.

The stories are just as spellbinding today as they were in those far-off days, and are here presented in simple text so that younger readers can enjoy them.

Adapted from Aladdin and Ali Baba in the standard Ladybird edition
0 7214 7501 9

Aladdin
Ali Baba

retold by Marie Stuart

with illustrations by
Robert Ayton

Ladybird Books Loughborough 1976

Aladdin and his wonderful lamp

Long ago, in China, there lived a tailor named Mustafa. He was very poor. He had a son called Aladdin.

Mustafa wanted Aladdin to learn how to make clothes so that he could help him. Aladdin did not want to. All he wanted to do was to play in the street with other boys.

Then his father fell ill and died. Aladdin's mother had to do all the work.

"I wish you would help me sometimes," she said. But he never did.

One day, when Aladdin was out playing, a man spoke to him.

"Do you know Mustafa the tailor?" he asked.

"He was my father," said Aladdin, "but he is dead. Did you know him?"

"He was my brother," the man replied.

"Then you are my uncle," said Aladdin.

"Yes," said the man. "I'm glad that I've found you. Tell your mother I shall come and see her soon."

When the man came to their house, Aladdin's mother said, "I did not know that my husband had a brother. He never talked about you."

The man was not really Aladdin's uncle but a MAGICIAN.

He said, "I left home a long time ago. Now that I have come back, I want to help you both." He smiled as he spoke.

"What work do you do?" he asked Aladdin.

"He just plays with the other boys all day," replied Aladdin's mother.

"It is time you did some work," said his uncle. "Would you like me to buy you some new clothes first?"

"I would like that," answered Aladdin.

Next morning the Magician took Aladdin shopping, and bought him some new clothes.

Next day, they went to look at big houses with lovely gardens. Aladdin liked them very much.

"One day I shall buy you a big house with a garden," promised the Magician. "Now let us sit and have something to eat. We have walked a long way."

The Magician had a bag of cakes and sweets and gave Aladdin as much as he could eat. Then he said, "I want you to see the best garden of all before we go back."

"Is it a long way?" asked Aladdin. "I don't think I can walk much more."

"We shall soon be there," said the Magician. So they walked on again until suddenly he cried, "Stop! This is the place."

"I don't see a garden," said Aladdin.

"You soon will," replied the Magician. He lit a fire and put something on it that made black smoke.

All at once, under his feet, Aladdin saw a big stone with a ring in it.

"Pull that ring," said the Magician.

Aladdin pulled, and up came the stone. Then he saw that it had been on top of a well.

It was very black inside the well and he did not like the look of it.

"You must go down," said the Magician.

"Will you come?" Aladdin asked.

"No. No one but you must go," replied the Magician. "But if you do everything I say, you will be very rich."

"All right! Just tell me what to do then," said Aladdin.

The Magician replied, "When you go down, you will find a door. Open it and go through. You will come to a very big cave and you will see some boxes with money in them. Do not take any of the money."

"How can I get rich if I don't take any?" asked Aladdin.

"Do as I say!" the Magician answered angrily. "Go straight through the big cave with money in it, and into the next cave. There you will see boxes overflowing with gold and silver, but do not take any. Walk straight through this cave to the end. Don't forget, you must not take any of the money, nor the gold and silver."

The Magician seemed to be growing taller and taller. He stared down at Aladdin as he spoke.

"When you come out of the cave of gold and silver you will see a fine garden. At the end of the garden you will see a table with a lamp on it. Bring the lamp to me.

"You can have anything you wish from the garden," said the Magician. "There are many beautiful things in it."

Then he took off a ring and gave it to Aladdin.

"This may be of use if you need help," he added. "Now go !"

Aladdin went down into the dark well. Down, down he went! At last he came to the bottom. It was dark and cold, but there was a door in front of him, just as the Magician had said.

He opened it and went through into a big cave, full of money. Aladdin walked straight past it, just as the Magician had told him to.

The next cave had the gold and silver in it, but again he did not take any.

He touched nothing there and went through a door into the garden.

There was the lamp on a table at the end
of the garden, just as the Magician had
told him it would be. He picked it up and
then looked around. He could not believe
his eyes!

On every tree he saw what looked like
little fires; but they were rich jewels - red,
blue, green, gold and white. And there were
so many of them!

He put down the lamp and took as many
of the jewels as he could carry.

Even when he could carry no more, there were still many left on the trees.

"I shall come back again one day," he thought, "but now I must take this lamp to my uncle."

So he left the garden and went back the way he had come. He was carrying so many jewels that he could only walk very slowly.

When he got to the top of the well he could see the Magician.

"Help me out, please!" he called up to him.

"Give me the lamp first," said the Magician, "then you can use both hands."

Aladdin was cunning. "No! I shall give it to you when I get out," he answered.

When the Magician saw that Aladdin would not let him have the lamp first, he was very angry.

He put something on the fire again and said some magic words.

At once the stone moved back into place over the top of the well. Aladdin was under it and could not get out. He was very frightened, for the stone was much too heavy for him to move by himself.

"Uncle! Uncle! I will give you the lamp if only you will help me out," he called. There was no answer. The Magician had gone.

When Aladdin found that it was no use calling, he climbed down the well again and tried to go back into the garden. The door was locked! No matter how hard he pushed, he could not open it.

He sat down in the darkness and cried. It was cold and wet. For three days he had nothing to eat or drink.

"I wish I had a little fire to warm me!" he said.

He rubbed his hands and, as he did so, he rubbed the ring that the Magician had given him.

"What do you want?" said a voice in the darkness. "I am the Slave of the Ring. I will come whenever you rub the ring and do anything you ask." Aladdin stared through the darkness, but could see nothing.

"What do you want?" asked the voice again.

"Please take me home," begged Aladdin, who was too cold and hungry to feel frightened.

No sooner had he said this than he found that he was home!

His mother cried, "Here you are at last! I thought you were lost!"

She gave him something to eat and drink and he went to bed.

Next day she said, "There is nothing left in the house for us to eat. I must work to get some more money."

Aladdin said, "It will take a long time, and I am hungry now. I shall go to the shop and ask a man I know to buy this lamp from me."

"It looks so old," replied his mother. "Let me give it a rub first. I shall soon make it look like new. Then you will get more money for it."

She took the lamp and gave it a hard rub with a duster.

Suddenly there was a puff of smoke, and a strange-looking man appeared. He bowed and said, "I am the Slave of the Lamp."

Aladdin's mother jumped with fright, and the lamp fell from her hands.

"It's all right, Mother," cried Aladdin, picking up the lamp. "Don't be afraid!"

Then the strange man said, "The lamp you are holding is a magic one. Whenever you rub the lamp I will appear, and do whatever you ask."

As they were both very hungry, Aladdin said, "Please will you bring us something to eat and drink."

The Slave of the Lamp clapped his hands and a fine dinner was set before them. The table was loaded with every sort of tasty food you could think of. Even the cups and plates were made of gold.

The Slave of the Lamp left them to enjoy the feast.

Aladdin did not realise the magical power of the lamp. So when they needed some more food, he said, "I will take these plates to the shop. The money I get for them will last us for a long time."

For some time, they were very happy and had everything they wished for.

But the time came when they had used up all the money. Suddenly Aladdin thought, "Perhaps I could rub the lamp again."

He rubbed the lamp and at once the Slave appeared and gave him everything he and his mother needed.

Whenever they wanted anything, they had only to rub the lamp, and the Slave gave them all they asked for.

Aladdin's mother was very pleased, for she no longer had to go out to work to get money for food. She had a large house, and plenty of money to buy all the food and fine clothes that she could ever wish for.

For some years, Aladdin and his mother enjoyed all the good things the Slave of the Lamp brought them. During this time, Aladdin grew into a very handsome young man.

One day when Aladdin was walking in the street, he saw a Princess going by on horse-back.

As soon as he saw her, he fell in love with her. She was the most beautiful girl he had ever seen.

"I want to marry the Princess," he told his mother when he got home.

"We must ask the King," she replied. "The jewels you found would make a good gift for him."

Aladdin's mother took a bag full of jewels to the King. Handing him the bag, she said, "My son loves the Princess and wants to marry her."

"What wonderful jewels," cried the King.

"Your son must be a very important man."
Then he promised that Aladdin could marry
the Princess.

Aladdin's mother went home to tell him
the good news.

But a rich man went to the King.
"My son will give you much more if he can
marry your daughter," he said.

Next day the people were told that the
Princess was to marry the rich man's son.
When Aladdin heard, he rubbed the lamp.

The Slave appeared and Aladdin said
angrily, "Bring the Princess and the rich
man's son to me at once."

Soon the Slave was back with them.
The man was shut in a dark room.

Then Aladdin spoke to the Princess, "Do not be afraid. I have brought you here to tell you that your father promised that you could marry me."

He told the Princess of his love for her.

Then the Slave took her and the rich man's son back to the palace.

The rich man's son was very frightened. He told his father and the King that he no longer wanted to marry the Princess.

The Slave returned to Aladdin to tell him what had happened.

Then Aladdin said to the Slave, "Bring me many bags of gold and jewels, and some slaves to carry them to the King."

Off went the slaves and Aladdin's mother to the Palace.

When the King looked inside the bags of gold and jewels, he was delighted.

"NOW will you let the Princess marry my son?" asked Aladdin's mother.

"Yes. Tell him to come here at once,"
replied the King.

Before Aladdin went to see the King, he
said to the Slave, "Bring me rich new
clothes and a fine, white horse."

When the Princess saw Aladdin on his
horse she fell in love with him at once.

"Before I marry her, I must have a house
to take her to," said Aladdin to the King.
"Where would you like it to be?"

"You could build a house near the Palace," said the King. "The Queen would like that."

"It shall be done," promised Aladdin.

Then the happy Aladdin went back home.

That night he rubbed the lamp. He said to the Slave, "Make me the best house that anyone has ever seen. You must put in it the best beds, chairs and tables, and the best pictures. Let there be flowers in all the rooms."

The Slave left to do as Aladdin asked.

Next morning the house was ready.
It was close to the Palace, just as the King
had asked. It was much nicer than the
King's own palace. Everything in it was of
the best.

So Aladdin married the Princess and they
went to live in their new home.

Aladdin's mother was glad her son was
so happy. She liked the Princess very much.

All was well for a year or two.
Then one day the Magician came back.

When he found that Aladdin was now a
Prince, the Magician was very cross.

"It's because he has the magic lamp,"
he thought. "I must get it away from him."

The Magician thought for a long time.
Suddenly he had a clever idea.

He went to a shop to buy some new
lamps. Then he walked up and down the
streets calling out, "New lamps for old!
New lamps for old!"

When the women heard the Magician

calling they came running out of their houses to change their old lamps for new ones.

The Princess heard about the wonderful bargain. She thought, "Aladdin has an old lamp in his bedroom. He will be pleased to get a new one for it."

The Princess did not know it was a magic lamp, so she changed it for a new one.

Aladdin had gone away for a few days. If he had been there he would never have let her change his lamp.

As soon as the Magician had the lamp in his hand, he took it to a place where no one could see him and gave it a rub.

When the Slave appeared he told him, "Take the house of Aladdin, and all that is in it, away from here and put it down near my home in Africa."

The Slave waved his hand, and the next moment Aladdin's house, with all the beautiful things and the Princess inside it, disappeared.

When the sun came up the next morning, the King and Queen saw that Aladdin's house was no longer there. Where it had stood, there was a large empty field.

Where could it be ? No one could tell them. They did not know what to do about it, and the Queen was very worried. "What has happened to my daughter ?" she cried.

"Where is Aladdin ?" shouted the King. "Find him at once and bring him to me. We must get the Princess back."

The King's men rushed off to look for Aladdin. They searched in every town and village, all over the country.

At last they found Aladdin. They pulled him from his horse and took him to the King.

"Where is the Princess?" cried the King.

"She is at home," Aladdin replied.

"But where is your home?" asked the King.

"What do you mean?" said Aladdin. Then he saw that his house was not there any more.

"Bring the Princess back or you must die," cried the King.

Aladdin ran out to get his lamp. But he could not find it because his house had gone.

He sat down to think. Then he remembered his magic ring. He gave it a rub. At once the Slave of the Ring stood before him.

"Take me to the Princess," said Aladdin.

Suddenly he was in his house with the Princess. Looking through the window he saw a desert. The house was in Africa!

The Princess told him that the Magician had given her a new lamp for the old one that had been in the bedroom.

Then Aladdin said, "This man says he is my uncle, but he is really a wicked Magician. I must get the lamp away from him quickly, so that we can go back home."

"He is staying near here," said the Princess. "I saw him ride by yesterday on a camel."

Aladdin gave the Princess a little bag, and said to her, "Tomorrow you must ask the Magician to supper. When he is not looking, empty this bag into his cup. Don't put any of it into your own cup."

Next day the Princess waited by the window until she saw the Magician riding along on his camel. Then she went out to meet him, and asked him to supper.

Later on, she made lots of nice things to eat, and laid the table with gold dishes.

The Magician came to supper and the Princess did as Aladdin had told her. When the Magician drank from his cup, he fell back dead.

The lamp dropped to the floor. Aladdin picked it up and gave it a rub.

When the Slave appeared, Aladdin ordered, "Take us, and our home, back to where it was before."

Next moment, the desert outside the window disappeared from view. The Princess smiled happily as she saw they were back in their own country.

When the King looked out of the palace window, he was delighted to see Aladdin's house back where it had been.

"Look!" he said to the Queen, excitedly. "The Princess and Aladdin are back! Let us go over to see them at once."

They went over as fast as they could, and the Princess ran out to meet them.

"I am so glad to be back," she cried. "It was terrible living so far away, and I missed you both very much."

The Queen put her arms round her daughter. "Never mind, you're safe at home now."

"A wicked Magician took me away but he is dead now," the Princess told them. "Dear Aladdin found me. I love him very much and I am very happy."

The King and Queen were grateful to Aladdin, and they all lived happily ever after.

Ali Baba
and the forty thieves

Once there were two
brothers, one called Cassim,
and one called Ali Baba. When
they grew up, Cassim married a woman
who was rich, but Ali Baba married a
woman who had no money at all.

Each day Ali Baba went out with his
three little donkeys to cut down trees for
firewood. Then he took the wood round the
streets to sell it.

This was how he made his living, but he
never had much money.

One day, when he was at work in the woods, Ali Baba saw a big cloud of dust in the distance. As he watched, it came nearer and nearer.

"It is men on horseback," he thought.

Then the horsemen came into view, and he did not like the look of them at all. He said to his donkeys, "I don't want these men to see me. They may take my wood. You go off so that they will not see you and I will climb up into this tree. I will call you when they have gone."

Up into the tree he went and on came the men. Then the first man said: "Stop! The place is over there!"

Ali Baba stayed as quiet as he could, and wondered what was going to happen. He certainly did not want these men to know he was there!

All the men jumped from their horses and Ali Baba saw that every horse had a big sack on its back. The men fed the horses, then lifted these sacks off the horses' backs and put them on their own backs. Ali Baba thought the sacks looked very heavy.

When the horses had finished eating, they were led away and the men walked up to a big rock that was near Ali Baba's tree.

Ali Baba counted the men as they stood nearby. There were forty of them.

Standing in front of the big rock, one of the men called, "Open Sesame!"

Ali Baba saw a door in the rock open! The man went in and all the others went in after him, then the door closed again.

"I wish I could get down now and run off home," said Ali Baba, "but they might come out again soon and see me."

So he still sat in the tree. He wondered why he had never seen the door in the rock before! Who had opened it? Was it the entrance to a cave?

And why were the men taking those sacks into it? They were such big sacks—what was in them? Could it be money? Were the men robbers? If so, it would be dangerous to climb down.

At last the men came out, and they did not have any sacks with them. When all of them were out, the head man called, "Close Sesame!"

The door in the rock closed. Then they went to their horses, jumped on their backs and were off and away!

Ali Baba came down from the tree as fast as he could. He went to the rock and called "Open Sesame!" just as the man had done. At once the door opened and Ali Baba looked into a cave. In it there were not only the sacks which the robbers had left, but gold, silver, jewels and silks, too.

There was no time to be lost. If the men came back and found him they would kill him. So he went in quickly to have a good look around.

All of the sacks left by the men were full of money!

He soon pulled the biggest sacks of money up to the door. It had closed after him when he went in, but when he called, "Open Sesame!" it opened at once to let him go out.

Then he said, "Close Sesame!" and it closed.

It did not take him long to find his three donkeys. He put the sacks on their backs with some wood on top, so that no one would know the sacks were there. Then he went home.

His wife did not know what to think when she saw all the money in the sacks. He told her where he had found it but said she must not tell anyone.

"Where will you keep it?" she asked.

"I will dig a pit and put it there," he said.

"First let me see how much there is," she said as she put her hand into one of the sacks. She picked up a handful of coins and started to count them.

"Stop! It will take too long," said Ali Baba. "There are too many to count them all."

"You dig the pit, and I will go to Cassim's house and ask him to let us have a box to put them in," said his wife. "I want to know how much there is."

"Don't tell them why you want it," said Ali Baba, as she went away.

Cassim was not at home. He was at his shop, but his wife was in the house.

"What do you want a box for?" she asked.

"To put some flour in," replied Ali Baba's wife. "And could you let me have a cup as well? I want to see how much we have."

As she went to get the cup she thought, "How can Ali Baba's wife have so much flour? They have very little money to buy any. I must find out what she is up to. I know what to do!"

She put some wax on the bottom of the cup where it could not be seen.

Ali Baba's wife hurried home as fast as she could with the box and cup.

"I will see how much money it takes to fill this cup," she said. "Then we can see how many cups will fill the box. That way, we can find out how much money we have."

She gave the cup to Ali Baba, and he started to count the money. He filled the cup, and poured the coins into the box, then filled the cup again.

They found forty cups of money would go into the box, and they could fill the box three times from one sack. But they had three sacks! What a lot of money! And all gold! How pleased they were.

"Now I must take the cup back," said Ali Baba's wife.

She did not know that a gold coin was
stuck to the wax on the bottom of the cup.
Cassim's wife soon found it, and when her
husband came home from his shop she said,
"Have you any money?"

"No," said Cassim. "I did not sell much
today."

"Ali Baba has some," said his wife.

Cassim looked at her in amazement. He
could not believe his ears!

"What are you saying, woman?" he asked. "You know Ali Baba has no money."

His wife began to laugh as she saw his face. "Aha! He has more than you have," she said. "He has so much gold that he keeps it in a big box. He has so much that he cannot count it properly!"

Then she told Cassim how she had found this out. Cassim was not at all pleased and went to Ali Baba's house to ask him where he had got the gold.

"How do you know that I have some money?" asked Ali Baba.

When Cassim told him how his wife had found out, Ali Baba said, "All right, I will tell you about it."

But Cassim was greedy. He did not want to have less money than Ali Baba. So he said, "You must take me to the place where the gold is. If you don't, I will go to the police and tell them that you are a robber."

Ali Baba did not want his brother to go to the police, so he said, "I will tell you how to find your way to the cave."

He took his brother outside, and pointed out which road to take. He told Cassim that the cave was quite a long way away, and that he had found it when cutting firewood.

Then he told Cassim about the magic door. "When you get to the place you will see a tree with a big rock close by. Then you just say, 'Open Sesame!' and a door will open. When you come out say, 'Close Sesame!' This is all you have to do."

Next day as soon as the sun was up, Cassim went off on his horse. He took eight more horses with him to carry as much money as possible away from the cave. He soon found the right place and the door in the rock.

"Open Sesame!" he called and the door opened. Into the cave he went and the door closed after him. He looked round at all the sacks of gold and jewels. Which should he take? He pulled the biggest ones to the door.

"I don't think I can take any more this time," he said, when he had eight of them. "Now I must get away as fast as I can."

But he was thinking so much about what was in the sacks that he forgot how to open the door.

He knew the word was the name of some sort of seed, so he said "Open Wheat!" not "Open Sesame!" The door stayed closed.

Then he said: "Open Corn!" But that was not right. "Open Oats!" Nothing happened!

He tried and tried, but he just could not think of the right word.

Cassim grew afraid. He knew the robbers were all very cruel men, and he wished he had not been so greedy.

He went on trying to get out for a long, long time. At last he gave up and waited in fear for his life.

He was still there when the robbers came

to put more sacks in the cave. As they rode up to the door, they saw Cassim's horses nearby. They said to one another, "Someone must have found out how to get in. Don't let him get away!"

Then the head man called, "Open Sesame!"

As the door opened Cassim ran out. The robbers drew their swords and attacked him. Then they left him in the cave, thinking he was dead.

That night, Cassim's wife went to Ali
Baba and said, "Cassim has not come back.
Please try to find him."

So Ali Baba went to the cave and found
his brother there, nearly dead. He put him
on the back of his donkey and took him
home.

"We must not let anyone know about
this," Ali Baba said to Cassim's wife.

"We must tell people that Cassim is not well. My wife and I will come to your house to help look after him. But he is hurt so badly that we must get some help."

Morgiana, the girl who worked for Cassim's wife, said, "I know a wise old shoemaker who has made many sick people better. I shall need some money to pay him however."

Ali Baba gave her money to pay him.

Next morning, before the sun was up, and when no one was about in the streets, Morgiana went to the old man's shop.

The door was closed, and there was no one in sight.

She knocked at the door loudly and waited, but there was no answer. Morgiana grew worried. Where could the old man be?

At last she heard footsteps, and the shoemaker opened the door. He was surprised to see her. "What do you want so early in the day?" he asked.

Morgiana said, "Will you come to our house, please? Someone is very ill. I will give you this money if you will help us."

"Where is your house?" said the old man.

"I cannot tell you," said Morgiana. "You must not see where it is. So close your eyes and keep them closed all the time I am taking you there."

She led him to Cassim's house and up to his bedroom. Then she said, "You may open your eyes now. Can you do anything to save this man's life?"

The wise old man looked at Cassim. He shook his head and said, "This man is very ill, but I will do my best."

The old man bandaged Cassim's wounds, made him a special drink and watched over him for many hours. But the cruel robbers had done their work too well. Nothing would make Cassim better. At last the old man said, "I can do no more to help this man!"

Then Morgiana said to him, "Thank you for all you have done. Now I will take you back to your shop, but do not tell anyone that you have been here. Now close your eyes again until I tell you to open them."

The old man closed his eyes and Morgiana took him back to his shop. Two days later Cassim died. Morgiana ran into the street calling, "My master is dead! My master is dead!"

The women came out of their houses to see who was calling. They also saw Cassim's wife at the bedroom window, crying. Next day, Cassim's body was taken outside the city and buried.

After that, Ali Baba and his wife went to live with Cassim's wife in her house, and Ali Baba's son went to work in Cassim's shop.

Three or four days later, the robbers went back to the cave. When they opened the door in the rock they saw that Cassim was no longer there.

"Someone must have taken him away," they said. "One of us must go and find out who it is because whoever did it must know about our cave."

"I will go," said one of the men.

Off he went. Next morning, he came to
the street where the old man had his shop.
He was sitting at his door with a shoe in his
hand.

"Do many people come to you for shoes,
old man?" said the robber.

"Yes," said the old man, "And they come
for other things too. Only the other day I was
asked to save the life of a man who had
been stabbed and was nearly dead. It was
too late—I could do nothing for him."

"What!" said the robber. "Take me to the house where you went and I will give you this bag of gold."

"I don't know where the house is," replied the old man, "because I had to keep my eyes closed all the way. A girl took me."

"Then see if you can find it with your eyes closed," said the robber. "You must know if you went right or left, and whether it was a little way or a long way. Come on, give me your hand and close your eyes."

They set off hand in hand, walking very slowly. From time to time the old man paused, but each time the robber hurried him on. At last they came to Cassim's house.

"I think this is the right place," said the old man, stopping in front of the door.

The robber made a white cross on the door. Then he took the old man back to his shop, gave him the bag of gold and went away.

When Morgiana went out shopping, she saw the white cross on their door, and wondered what it meant.

"Who put this there?" she thought. "It
could have been the children, but I don't
think so. I don't like this. Why is it only on
our house and not on the others?" So she
made some more white crosses on the
doors of the other houses. Then she went
on to do her shopping.

By this time the robber had gone back to
the cave.

"I have found the house where the man lives," he said to the others. "Come with me and I will take you to it."

But when they got there he found so many houses with a white cross on the door that he could not tell which was the right one. There was nothing they could do but go back to the cave again, to tell the robber chief.

Then another man said, "Let me try."

So the next day the old man went with him as he did with the first man. When they found the house, a red cross was marked on the door by the robber.

"All the others have a white cross," he said. "This will be the only one with a red cross."

Morgiana saw the red cross when she came back from the shops. So she put some red crosses on the doors of other houses, just as she had done with the white crosses before.

When the robbers came again they still could not tell which was the right house, because nearly all the houses had a red cross on the door.

"This will not do!" said the robber chief, becoming very angry. "I must go and find the house myself!"

So he went and found the old man who took him to the house as he had done with the other two men. The head man did not put a cross on it. He had a good hard look at it and went away.

"I must think what to do next," he said to the robbers when he got back. "Now that we know where Ali Baba lives, we can make sure that he never comes to our cave again!"

Next day he said, "I have it! You must go and buy some big jars—the kind they use for oil. But I want oil in only one of them. The others must have nothing in them."

"Why do you want empty jars?" said one of the robbers.

"Because you are going to hide in the jars when you have put them on the horses' backs. I shall take the horses to Ali Baba's house. I shall tell him I have come a long way, and I shall ask him to let me sleep at his house for the night."

The robber chief smiled as he spoke. He knew it was a very good plan.

"What about us?" said the men.

"You will have to stop in the jars. They are so big there will be plenty of room in them for you. When the time comes I shall tell you what to do."

Things went just as the robber chief had hoped. Ali Baba welcomed him to his house and agreed that he could stay for the night, just as he did for anyone who had travelled from far away places.

Ali Baba helped him to take the jars down from the horses' backs. Then he said, "Come in now and have a good dinner." He took the robber chief inside.

After the robber had eaten and drunk all he could, he said, "I must go now and give the horses some water. They too have come a long way, carrying my jars of oil."

While he was in the stable, he went to each jar and spoke to the man who was in it. He was careful to speak very quietly, in case any of Ali Baba's servants were near.

"When I make a call like a bird from my window," he said, "you must get out of your jars. I shall come down and tell you what to do."

Then he went back into the house, rubbing his hands with glee. Tonight would see the end of Ali Baba, and the secret of the robbers' cave would be safe!

When Morgiana went to make up the fire for the night, her lamp went out and she could not see what she was doing.

"I must buy some more oil in the morning," she said, "but tonight I shall take some from one of those jars."

She went to the first jar, and the man who was in it, thinking she was the robber chief, said, "Is it time?"

This made her jump, but she quickly replied in a deep voice, "Not now. Soon..."

She went to the next jar and the next. Every time the man who was in it said, "Is it time?" And Morgiana replied, "Not now. Soon!"

Morgiana was very clever, and as she went round all the jars she thought of a plan to get rid of the robbers.

The last jar had oil in it and she put some in her lamp. Then she filled her biggest kettle with oil and put it on the stove to heat. When it boiled, she tipped some into each of the jars. And that was the end of the robbers!

When the robber chief came down in the night he found his men all dead. So he jumped on his horse and quickly rode away.

Next morning Morgiana told Ali Baba what had happened and about the crosses on the door. He thanked her and said he would never forget what she had done.

Then he asked some of his men to dig a big hole in the woods. That night they put the dead robbers in it.

Morgiana was still worried. It was true the robbers could no longer hurt anyone, but what of their chief? He had escaped!

The robber chief was not far away, but he was now alone. So he said, "I shall buy a shop. In it I shall put the silks and jewels that are in the cave. If I sell them I can make a good living."

He did so and everyone said what a good shop it was.

One day, Ali Baba's son met the robber chief. Their shops were near to one another. He asked the robber to come home with him for a meal.

Ali Baba did not remember what the robber chief looked like, but when Morgiana saw him she thought, "That man has been here before. He means to do something bad. I must stop him."

So she said to Ali Baba, "When dinner is over, shall I come in and dance for you?" Ali Baba said that she could, and after the meal was finished Morgiana came into the room and began to dance gracefully in front of the robber chief.

When she had finished her dance, Morgiana went round the room holding out a cup for them to put money into. Ali Baba gave her some and so did his son.

Then she came to the robber chief. As he put some money in the cup, she saw that he had a knife hidden in his clothes.

Morgiana knew now that this was the robber chief. Unless she did something quickly, they would all die.

Before the robber chief could stop her, she snatched the knife and killed him with it.

"What have you done?" cried Ali Baba, jumping up.

"If I had not done that," replied Morgiana, "he would have killed you. He is the robber chief who came here with the jars of oil."

Looking at the robber chief, Ali Baba saw that Morgiana was right.

"You are a good girl," he said. "I am so
pleased with you that I shall be happy if you
will marry my son."

So Morgiana and Ali Baba's son were
married. When they needed money, they
went to the cave and used the robber's
treasure. But they made sure that most of
it was given to the poor.

So everything ended well for everyone
but the robbers!